SOMETH
MUST BE
WRONG
WITH ME

*Dedicated to
Steve Siler and
Stephen Breithaupt—
great men with tender hearts.*

Dino could hardly wait until school was over so he could go to the gym. Since the after-school activities program began, he could play basketball every day with his new friend, Coach Tom. Dino knew Coach liked him because he let him stay and help put things away at the end of practice.

The best thing was that Coach was interested in everything that had happened at school that day. Dino missed his dad since his parents' divorce, but it helped to feel special to Coach Tom. Coach and his wife lived near Dino's home, so every day when the work was done at the gym, Coach drove Dino home.

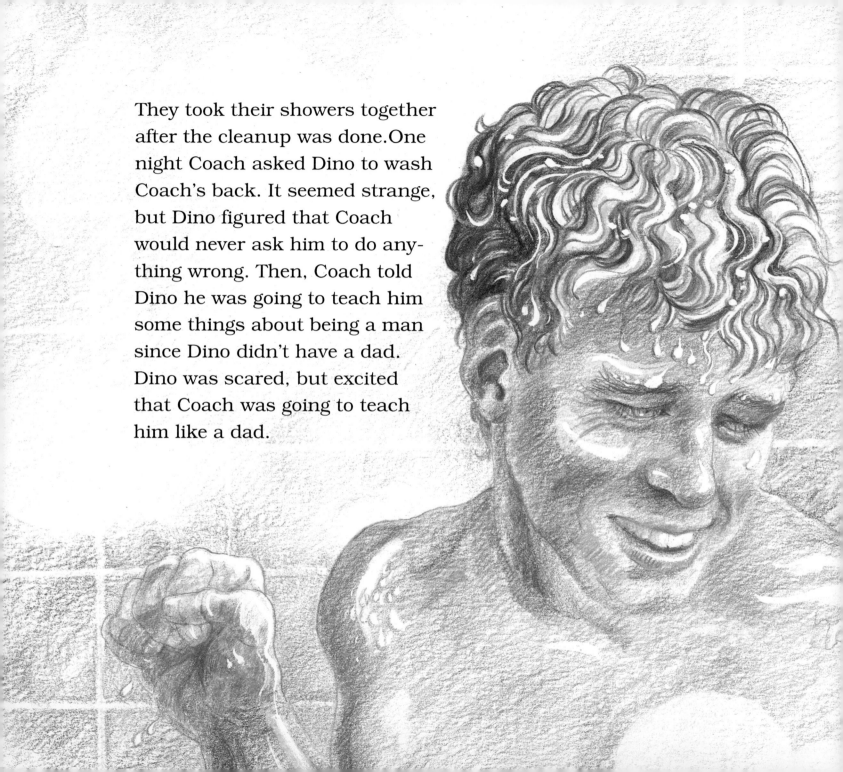

They took their showers together after the cleanup was done. One night Coach asked Dino to wash Coach's back. It seemed strange, but Dino figured that Coach would never ask him to do anything wrong. Then, Coach told Dino he was going to teach him some things about being a man since Dino didn't have a dad. Dino was scared, but excited that Coach was going to teach him like a dad.

Dino was confused when the bad stuff started happening. One day Coach said, "Most adults treat you like a kid, but I'm going to treat you like an adult." Once, when Dino backed away, Coach asked, "What's the matter, don't you trust me?" Dino didn't know WHAT to think. The special attention was nice, and Coach did say he wasn't going to hurt him and that this is what people did when they loved each other.

The day Coach brought his camera and took pictures of both of them in the shower, Dino was scared. Coach said, "Your mom wouldn't like this, so don't tell her."

No problem. He wasn't telling *anybody!* But then he began to have nightmares and he woke up sweating, screaming, and shaking several nights each week. He decided he didn't want to go to the gym anymore.

The next day he told his mom he didn't want to play basketball anymore. When he told her he'd rather go to the neighbor's house with his little brother, she got worried. She said, "Dino, something MUST be wrong. Can you tell me about it?" And before he could say "No," he started to cry.

"I'm sorry, Mom. Boys are supposed to be able to take care of themselves. At first it was fun to be with Coach. My teacher said to tell if a grown-up does bad things to you, but I was scared to say anything, Mom."

By now Dino was sobbing and Mom was mad. Dino thought she was mad at *him*, but she told him she was just mad at what had happened.

Dino ran to his room. To his surprise, there on the window ledge was a beautiful white dove who spoke gently,

"It's not wrong to like the special attention, Dino. You aren't old enough to always understand if what an adult is doing is right. Coach offered you something that seemed too good to turn down, and he wanted you to pay a price that was too high to pay.

"When you need a hug, you can ask for one, no strings attached. You don't have to share your body."

And with that, the dove flew away.

When Mom came to Dino's bedroom, she said, "I'm upset, but not with you, and I am sad and that's okay. I will be able to take care of you. What are you worried about now?"

"Mom, please don't TELL anybody...please!"

"Son, I know it took a lot of courage for you to tell me what Coach did to you. I'm sorry that I didn't know this was happening. Now I understand why you have been fighting so much with your brother.

"I called the police and they will send a social worker or police officer to talk with you. They said you will probably need to have a doctor examine your body, even the parts that were sexually abused. We need to be sure everything is okay. The doctor's touching is for your health, and is okay."

His mom told him, "I know you are worried about talking to the police, but Dino, they are on YOUR side. They know you didn't do anything wrong."

"Could you help me tell the story, Mom? I won't know how to say it."

"No, Dino, you can tell it in your own words. They will ask you simple questions that will help you talk about it."

"You don't have to tell any of your friends. If they ask about it, you can say, 'I'd rather not talk about it.'

"You won't have to talk to Coach Tom. You might not even see him unless this goes to trial.

"But Dino, one other person who needs to know what has happened to you is your little brother. He deserves to know."

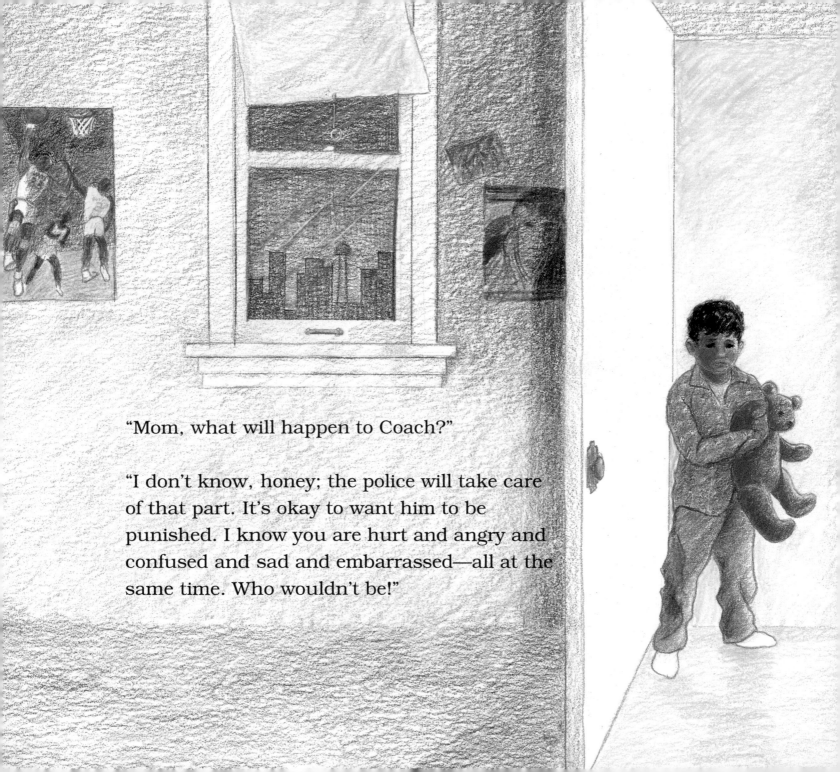

"Mom, what will happen to Coach?"

"I don't know, honey; the police will take care of that part. It's okay to want him to be punished. I know you are hurt and angry and confused and sad and embarrassed—all at the same time. Who wouldn't be!"

Mom left the room and
Dino sat quietly with
his head in his lap.

Just then he heard a gentle
tap, tap, tap—and there he
was again, the amazing dove.
This time the dove marched
up beside Dino and said, "My
name is LOVE-DOVE. I know
what has happened to you. It's
okay to like someone and be
angry with them at the same
time.

"I know you wanted the abuse to stop, and that you didn't want to get anybody in trouble, but telling was the only way to make it stop. It's not your fault that Coach Tom needs help with his problem. Now he has a chance to get the help he needs."

"LOVE-DOVE, did he pick me because there was something *different* about me?"

"No, dear Dino, he picked you because you were there. He was looking for a boy your age."

And with that, the dove was gone again.

The meeting with the social worker and the policeman was tape-recorded. They said if this went to a trial, Dino could listen to the tape again before he had to testify. Dino asked if taping the interview meant that it would be on TV. The answer was "no"!

After the policeman left, the social worker stayed and talked about what would happen if Dino had to go to court.

She said, "What you told was important even if the coach doesn't go to jail.

"And if he doesn't go to jail, it doesn't mean the abuse didn't happen. If you go to court, the other lawyer will ask you questions you won't like, but it's not because he is a mean person. It's just that it is his job. You don't have to answer anything you don't understand."

"The trial is not to decide if YOU did anything wrong. Everybody knows YOU didn't do anything wrong. The judge wears a funny-looking robe so everybody knows who he is."

The social worker also said:

1. If you cry in the courtroom, it's okay. Lots of people do.

2. You can carry a special picture of your mother in your pocket and remember that she loves you.

3. The other lawyers might glare at you, but you don't have to look at them. You can look at me, and I will smile at you.

Dino was worried about going to court but he was also worried about going to see the counselor for the first time. The counselor was a person who helped kids with their feelings. Dino would be in a group with other boys who had been sexually abused. He didn't KNOW this had happened to other boys. When he entered the office, the counselor shook his hand. That was good. He didn't want any strange man hugging him.

Each week when Dino went to the group, the counselor reminded them about the rules: no laughing at what someone else says, and no talking about others in the group when you are away from the group. Dino thought that was fair. He sure didn't want anybody talking about HIM outside the group!

When he got home from the group he went to the roof to meet LOVE-DOVE. He shared all he was learning, and LOVE-DOVE smiled and sometimes he pranced when he was REALLY pleased!

Dino said, "I know that some people can't be trusted, such as people who trick you by saying that something is right when your parents tell you it's wrong. I know I can trust my feelings. If I feel uncomfortable around someone, I can *tell* someone."

It was easy to talk to LOVE-DOVE. It was almost as if he already knew how Dino felt before Dino spoke.

"LOVE, do you know that sexual abuse doesn't cause homo-sexuality? Not even if it felt good!"

"I know, Dino."

"And, LOVE, when people ask me why it took me
so long to share this or why I didn't run away,
I can say:

1. I didn't know it was abuse.
2. I was scared.
3. He was my friend.
4. I didn't want to get him in trouble."

"I know, Dino."

Now it was time for LOVE-DOVE to speak, and he said
softly, "Dino, you couldn't have done what you did one
minute sooner. You told when you were able to tell.

"And one more thing: Nobody can tell
by looking at you that you
were sexually abused."

That night Dino was sure his mother would want to talk to him about how angry he'd been lately. She did. Dino didn't know what to say. He didn't like what he was doing. And he was sure that his little brother wasn't too happy about being hit!

His mom said it was okay to feel angry but that he had a choice about what he would *do* with his anger. Hitting his brother was NOT an acceptable choice, but he COULD tear up newspapers and throw them real hard, or pound the clay she brought him. She also said he could write a letter to Coach Tom and tell him how much he hurt him. He didn't have to send the letter.

Then his mom said, "Dino, these bad feelings won't last forever. Getting well means someday you won't be making choices based on the abuse."

Dino had a lot to think about, so he tip-toed up to the roof where he knew LOVE would be waiting for him.

"LOVE-DOVE," Dino asked after awhile, "When someone hurts you REAL bad, do you have to forgive that person?"

"No, Dino, forgiveness is a choice. It doesn't mean that what he did to you was right. It doesn't mean he didn't hurt you! When you forgive a person it means that you let go of wanting to punish him. You are free to get on with your own life, even if he never says he is sorry.

"And, Dino, one more thing: When you are ready to forgive him, remember that you don't have to do this alone. I will help you, and I'm good at that kind of thing."

Dear Friend,

1. If you have been sexually abused, remember that the boy's experience is almost certainly different from your own.

2. Child molesters are single, married, heterosexual, homosexual, male and female.

3. Sexual abuse occurs in approximately one of every five boys, and the majority of boys who have been sexually abused know their molester.

4. Any child can be a victim: outgoing, talkative children as well as shy, quiet children; smart children and also slow children.

5. If the child tells you he has been abused, believe him; call the police, don't give the child a bath, and don't change his clothes if the abuse occurred that day.

6. After the crisis is over, children need language to talk about their bodies. Don't correct the child's language until after the legal proceedings are complete or it will appear you have coached him.